Felix's New Skirt

Kerstin Brichzin

with pictures by Igor Kuprin

minedition

Felix liked to wear skirts – the wider the better.
"My legs get a lot of air," he said.

"Can I wear your green dress?" Felix asked his sister Ava. "The one with the glittery flowers?"

"Only if I get your black jeans," Ava said, opening her wardrobe. Felix laughed and gave his sister a big hug.

"Mom," Ava called, "Felix needs his own dresses!"

"A red one!" Felix added, jumping on the bed with one of Ava's long dresses.

At the department store Felix tugged his mom toward the girls' clothes.

"Do you have red skirts?" he asked the salesperson. Felix pushed hangers with colorful clothes back and forth.

"Look, Mom!" Felix said when he found the perfect one.

His eyes shone as he held up a red pleated skirt.

"Well, let's see if it fits," Mom said, gently caressing his curly blond hair.

The salesperson smiled.

"You've got a beautiful girl," she said.

"Felix is a boy," Mom corrected her, "and he loves skirts."

Then the salesperson stopped smiling.

"Can I wear my new skirt to school tomorrow?" Felix asked.
 Dad wrinkled his forehead, looking serious. Mom and Ava were
 both quiet.
"Some people might not understand," Dad said, hugging him.
"I think you should wear pants for your first day."

Dad took Felix to school each morning, but each day Felix was less and less excited to go. "When can I wear my red skirt?" Felix asked, pulling at his jeans, twisting his mouth into a frown.

"Maybe... tomorrow," Dad whispered.

The next day Felix dashed out the front door in his red pleated skirt. Dad smiled uneasily and took his hand. When they arrived Felix exclaimed, "Look how my red skirt spins!" He was practically dancing.

But the other kids laughed at him. "You look like a girl!" they shouted, pointing at him. "Real boys don't wear dresses. Why don't you go play with someone else..."

"That's inappropriate," the other parents whispered to each other. "What kind of parent allows his child to do something like that?"

Felix was sad that no one wanted to play with him today. Raindrops pattered against the window, joining up and running down the glass. The other kids played together, but when they looked in Felix's direction, they pointed and giggled. He waited for the day to end with tears in his eyes.

Now Felix didn't feel like going to school anymore.
He wondered, *"Why don't they like my wonderful skirt? I can run faster and climb more easily. Why would they think Mom and Dad are bad? What have they done?"*

"It's not fair that girls are allowed to wear pants, but boys can't wear skirts," Felix told his Dad. "I should be able to wear whatever I like."

"You're right, Felix," his Dad said, "but other people aren't always so considerate."

Felix whispered, "Is there anything you can do to help me?"

Together they returned to the department store. "Do you have a long skirt in my size?" Felix's Dad asked the salesperson, winking at Felix.

Felix couldn't believe it.

For the next few days the two of them walked around town wearing their skirts. People glared at them and shook their heads. Felix just waved back and laughed.

One woman approached them, ranting: "You're wearing a skirt, you can't do that!" She stared at them for so long she stumbled into a street sign.

Felix gave her a hand. "Did you hurt yourself?" he asked.

"I'm okay," she said. "Are you a boy?"

"Sure!" Felix answered, taking his dad's hand.

The next morning Felix announced, "I want to go back to school. I'm ready." Mom and Ava both breathed a sigh of relief.

Dad walked Felix to school, as always.

"You're wearing a skirt, too?" one boy asked Felix's dad.

Dad nodded. "Today anybody can wear a skirt. Did nobody tell you?"

The boy shook his head with astonishment.

"You look funny in girl's cloths," another boy said to Felix.

"Is that bad?" Felix replied.

The boy shrugged his shoulders. "Boys have to wear pants. Only girls wear skirts."

"Isn't that unfair?" Felix said. "I want to wear what I like, and for me that's skirts and dresses." He gave his skirt a twirl.

From that day on no one asked if he was a boy or a girl. They simply called him Felix.